GOODNIGHT TOUCAN

Joanne Partis

LITTLE TIGER

LONDON

"Ta dah!"

Toucan had decided to throw
a sleepover party for his friends.
"It's going to be fabulous," he said.
"I hope everyone can come!"

Everyone was **excited** to receive their invitation.

"A sleepover party? Hooray!"

"How amazing!"

"Party . . . time!"

"Super cool!"

In fact, they were even **more** excited
than Toucan had expected.

"Yes please!" they all cried. "It's going
to be the best sleepover, ever!"

You hear that, Toucan?

Gulp!

Back at his treetop home, Toucan was starting to worry.
His decorations suddenly didn't feel special enough.
Not for the best sleepover **ever**!

"Not **yummy** enough!"

"Not **snuggly** enough!"

"Argh!!"
cried Toucan.
"I need to find things for the
perfect party – **pronto!**" And
off he charged into the jungle.

"Fabulous flower decorations!"
said Toucan. "Just what I need!"

The little yellow ones were pretty. Or the big pink ones?

Which ones do you think you can carry, Toucan?

"The biggest ones!" panted Toucan.

He was about to struggle home when he saw . . .

"Fluffy ferns! What a super snuggly bed they would make," cried Toucan.
He just had to have one.

Woah, Toucan!
Maybe that was a few too many.

"Huff . . .

   puff . . ." puffed Toucan.

He was furiously flapping to stay above the treetops.
But then he saw something really wonderful!
   "Oh my!" he said. "What a feast those yummy
bananas would make!"

Uh-oh! Maybe he should just get one or two?

Wow. What a lot of bananas!

"This sleepover is going to be the best after all!" Toucan huffed happily.

Night had fallen in the jungle, and the fireflies were coming out.

"Fairy lights!" gasped Toucan. "I must have them!"

The fireflies darted
here and there.

Toucan swooped . . .

. . . and then he dived!

Closer and closer and . . .

"Got you!" he cried. But uh oh . . .

Back at Toucan's house, it was sleepover time at last.

But Toucan was nowhere to be seen.

"We're here!" called Monkey.

"It's . . . bed . . . time!" yawned Sloth.

"I've brought bedtime stories!" said Tiger.

"Where are you, Toucan?" said Frog.

And **what** was that funny,

squelchy sound

coming from the jungle?

It **was** Toucan!

"Everything's **ruined**," wailed Toucan.
"It won't be the best sleepover ever!
I don't even have f-f-fairy lights."

"Yes **you** do!" said Frog, pointing to the twinkling stars.

"I love your decorations!" yawned Sloth.

"And I love your berries!" laughed Monkey.

"We've got **exactly** what we need to make this sleepover special," said Tiger.

"And

that

is . . ."

"You!" they all cried.
"Oh!" blushed Toucan.
Hadn't he been silly?

So Toucan snuggled up
with his very best friends
around him.

And that's all he really needed
for the best sleepover . . . ever!